P9-CDL-881

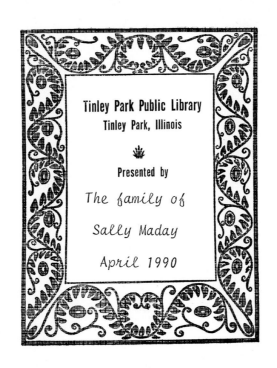

Tinley Park Public Library
Tinley Park, Illinois

Presented by

The family of

Sally Maday

April 1990

# The
# Wheels
## on the
# Bus

*To Alice Kovalski*

Copyright © 1987 by Maryann Kovalski
Musical notation by Miriam Katzin

All rights reserved. No part of this book may be reproduced in
any form or by any electronic or mechanical means, including
information storage and retrieval systems, without permission
in writing from the publisher, except by a reviewer who may
quote brief passages in a review.

First U.S. Edition

Library of Congress Cataloging-in-Publication Data
Kovalski, Maryann.
   The wheels on the bus.

   Summary: While a grandmother and grandchildren wait
for the bus, they sing the title song with such gusto they miss
their bus.
   1. Children's songs—Texts. [1. Buses—Songs and
music. 2. Songs] I. Title.
PZ8.3.K8535Wh   1987        [E]        87-3441
ISBN 0-316-50256-1

First published in Canada by Kids Can Press

Printed by Everbest Printing Co., Ltd., Hong Kong

# Maryann Kovalski

# The Wheels on the Bus

*Joy Street Books*
Little, Brown and Company
Boston          Toronto

One day, Grandma took Jenny and Joanna shopping for new winter coats.

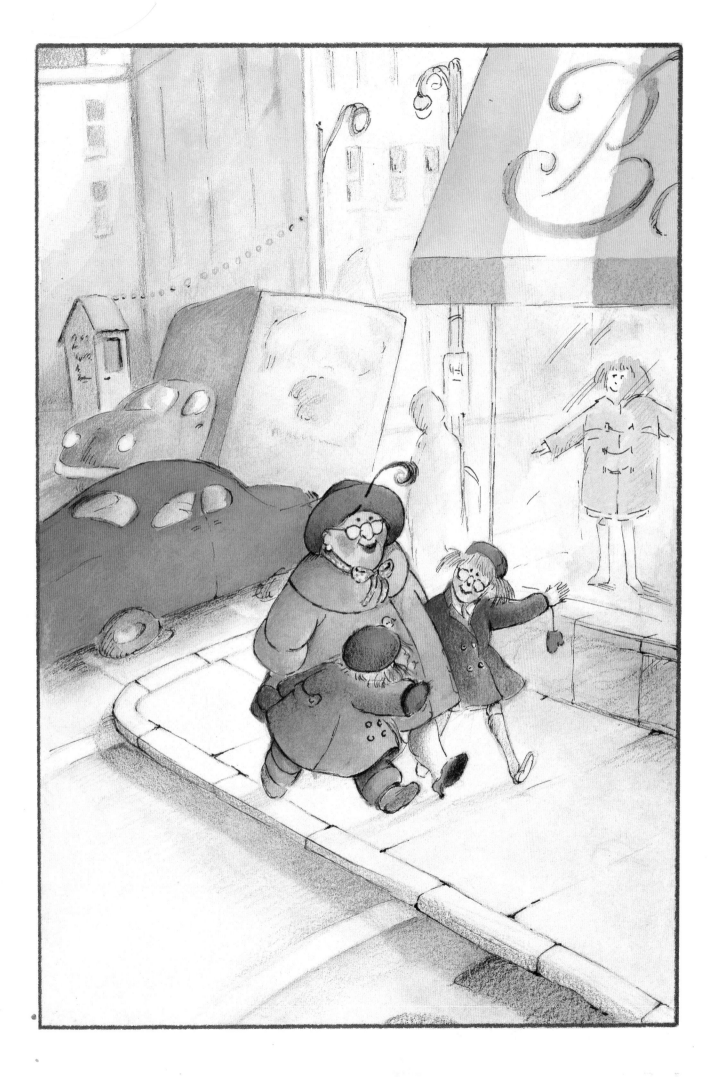

They tried on long coats and short coats,
blue coats and red coats, plaid coats and even
raincoats. Joanna chose a coat with wooden
barrel buttons. Jenny liked it too,
because of the hood.

When it was time to go home, the bus didn't come for a long time and everyone grew tired. "I have an idea, sweeties," said Grandma. "Let's sing a song my Granny sang with me when I was a little girl." And so they began to sing. . . .

The wipers on the bus go swish, swish, swish

swish, swish, swish

swish, swish, swish

The wipers on the bus go swish, swish, swish

all around the town.

The people on the bus hop on and off

on and off

on and off

The people on the bus hop on and off

all around the town.

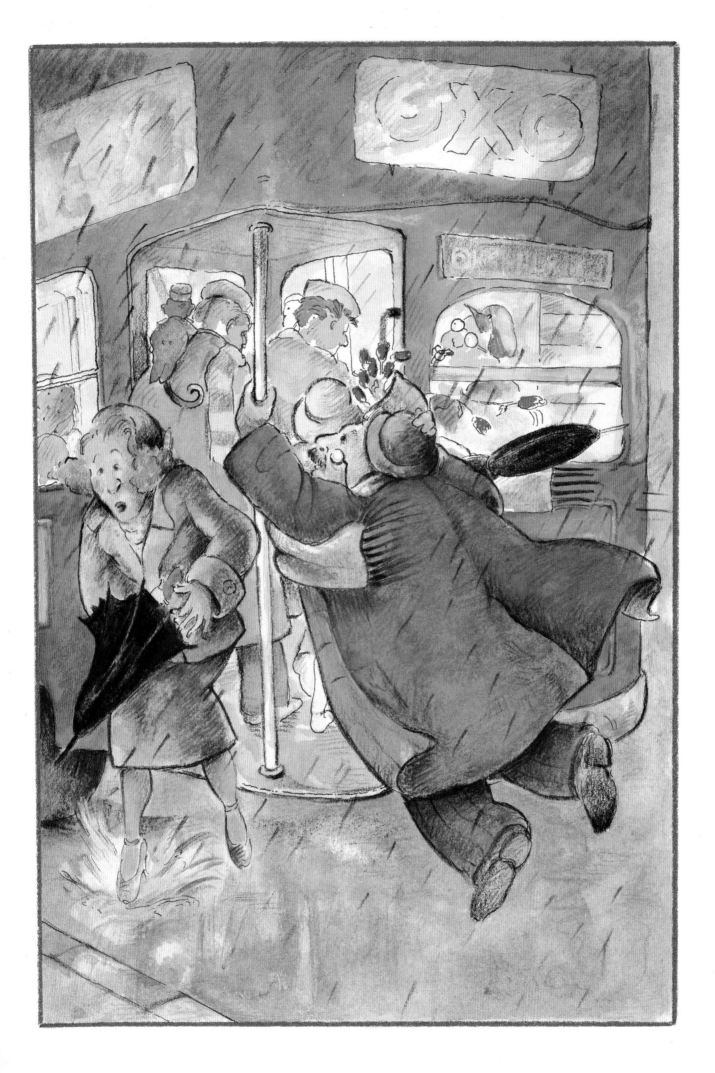

The horn on the bus goes toot, toot, toot

toot, toot, toot

toot, toot, toot

The horn on the bus goes toot, toot, toot

all around the town.

The money on the bus goes clink, clink, clink

clink, clink, clink

clink, clink, clink

The money on the bus goes clink, clink, clink

all around the town.

The people on the bus go up and down

up and down

up and down

The people on the bus go up and down

all around the town.

The babies on the bus go waaa, waaa, waaa

waaa, waaa, waaa

waaa, waaa, waaa

The babies on the bus go waaa, waaa, waaa

all around the town.

The parents on the bus go ssh, ssh, ssh

ssh, ssh, ssh

ssh, ssh, ssh

The parents on the bus go ssh, ssh, ssh

all around the town.

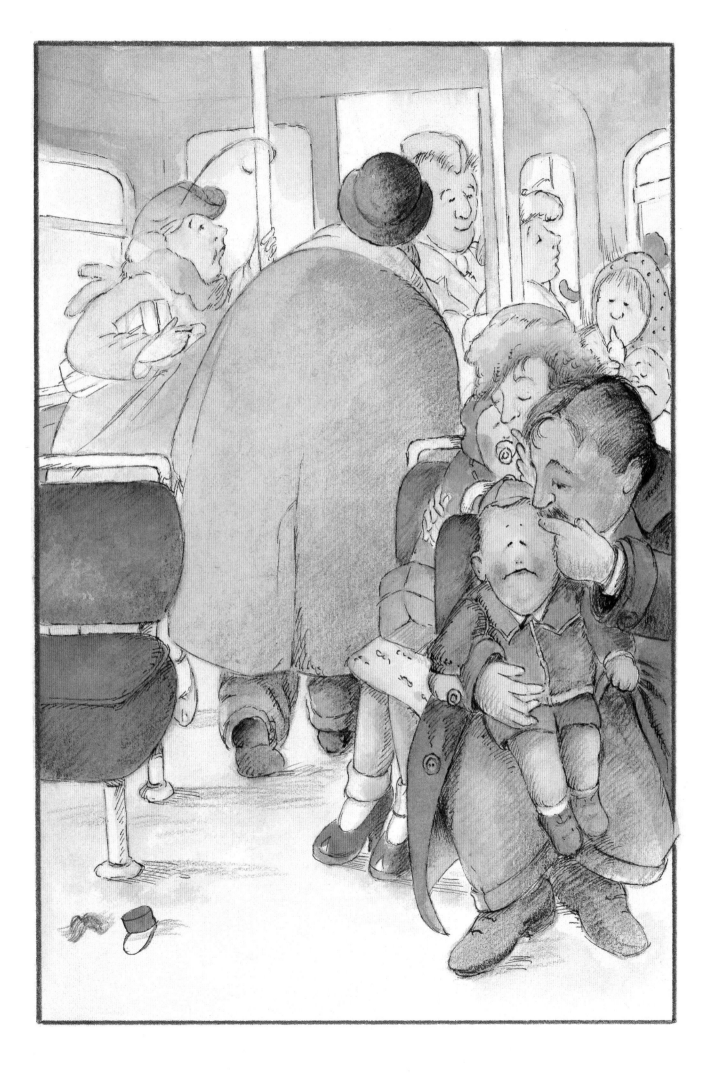

The wheels on the bus go round and round

round and round

round and round

The wheels on the bus go round and round

all around the town.

Grandma, Jenny, and Joanna had so much fun . . .

They missed the bus!

So . . .

They took a taxi.